For Hope Charlotte and family.
Grateful you popped up! —*A. D.*

For Jovita —*C. S.*

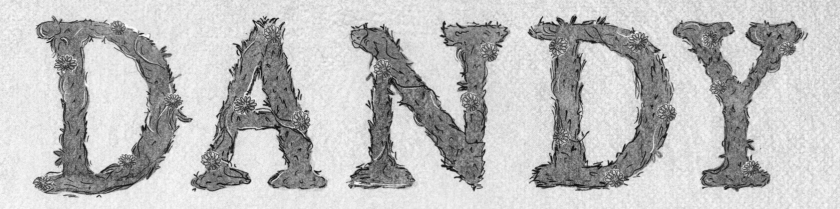

DANDY

Written by **Ame Dyckman** ❀ Illustrated by **Charles Santoso**

LITTLE, BROWN AND COMPANY

NEW YORK · BOSTON

Daddy spied something scary
on his perfect lawn.

He ran for his clippers. . . .

But he was too late.

"Hi, Daddy!"

"Sweetie!" Daddy said. "That's a weed!"

"A flower," Sweetie said. "Her name is Charlotte. She's my best friend."

Daddy hoped his friends wouldn't notice.

They did.

He tried during book time.

But Sweetie was there.

"Hi, Daddy!"

He tried during nap time.

But Sweetie was there.

"Hi, Daddy!"

He tried during snack time.

But Sweetie was there.

"Hi, Daddy!
We saved you a spot!"

Once again, Daddy hoped his friends wouldn't notice.

Daddy got serious.

But Sweetie was ALWAYS there.

"Hi, Daddy!"

Until it was time for swim lessons.

"Bye, Daddy! Take care of Charlotte!"

"I will!" Daddy said.

He couldn't wait.

But Daddy spied something else on his once perfect lawn: Sweetie's painting.

"I can't do it," Daddy cried.

WE KNOW!

(They were daddies, too.)

Then Daddy's snips . . . slipped.

"NOOOOO!" Daddy wailed.

"CHARLOTTE!"

They knew what they had to do.

Everyone hoped Sweetie wouldn't notice.

She did.

"Daddy!" Sweetie cried.
"There's something WRONG with Charlotte!"

"LOOK!"

Daddy looked at his lawn.

He looked at his little girl.

He chose.

"It'll be okay, Sweetie," Daddy said. "Watch."

And soon . . .

"Hi, Daddy!" Sweetie said.
"Meet Charlotte Two! And Charlotte Three!
And Charlotte Four! And . . ."

Sweetie beamed. "Aren't they beautiful?"

Daddy smiled. "Yes, Sweetie," he said.
"They're . . . DANDY."

AUTHOR'S NOTE

In our old neighborhood, the daddies took their lawn care VERY seriously.

When a dandelion popped up . . . WAR! WAR ON THE DANDELION!

We watched this instead of TV.

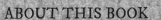

ABOUT THIS BOOK

The illustrations for this book were done digitally with handmade pencil textures on top. This book was edited by Mary-Kate Gaudet and designed by Jen Keenan. The production was supervised by Virginia Lawther, and the production editor was Marisa Finkelstein. The text was set in IM FELL DW Pica PRO, and the display type is hand-lettered by Jen Keenan.

Text copyright © 2019 by Ame Dyckman • Illustrations copyright © 2019 by Charles Santoso • Cover art copyright © 2019 by Charles Santoso. Cover design and lettering by Jen Keenan. • Cover copyright © 2019 by Hachette Book Group, Inc. • Hachette Book Group supports the right to free expression and the value of copyright. The purpose of copyright is to encourage writers and artists to produce the creative works that enrich our culture. • The scanning, uploading, and distribution of this book without permission is a theft of the author's intellectual property. If you would like permission to use material from the book (other than for review purposes), please contact permissions@hbgusa.com. Thank you for your support of the author's rights. • Little, Brown and Company • Hachette Book Group • 1290 Avenue of the Americas, New York, NY 10104 • Visit us at LBYR.com • First Edition: April 2019 • Little, Brown and Company is a division of Hachette Book Group, Inc. The Little, Brown name and logo are trademarks of Hachette Book Group, Inc. • The publisher is not responsible for websites (or their content) that are not owned by the publisher. • Library of Congress Cataloging-in-Publication Data • Names: Dyckman, Ame, author. | Santoso, Charles, illustrator. • Title: Dandy / written by Ame Dyckman; illustrated by Charles Santoso. • Description: First edition. | New York; Boston: Little, Brown and Company, 2019. | Summary: Although Sweetie has named and is caring for the sole dandelion on his perfect lawn, Daddy, with his friends' urging, does all he can to get rid of the weed before it spreads. • Identifiers: LCCN 2017051343| ISBN 9780316362955 (hardcover) | ISBN 9780316504959 (ebook) • Subjects: | CYAC: Fathers and daughters—Fiction. | Dandelions—Fiction. | Weeds—Fiction. | Neighborhood—Fiction. | Humorous stories. • Classification: LCC PZ7.D9715 Dan 2019 | DDC [E]—dc23 • LC record available at https://lccn.loc.gov/2017051343 • ISBNs: 978-0-316-36295-5 (hardcover), 978-0-316-50495-9 (ebook), 978-0-316-52763-7 (ebook), 978-0-316-52765-1 (ebook) • Printed in China • 1010 • 10 9 8 7 6 5 4 3 2 1